EROTICA 2 SECRETARY
THE PLEASURE OF SURRENDER

EROTICA BOOK 2

"We don't see things as they are.
We see things as we are."
Anaïs Nin, *The Seduction of the Minotaur (1961)*
Nicolas Blanc
Minuet Publishing

1

1. http://minuetpublishing.wix.com/books

CHAPTER 1. PERSONAL SECRETARY

"Jillian, please remove your dress for me," Olivia says looking up from her desk at her beautiful secretary.

Jillian Allesbury has a momentary look of uncertainty on her face.

The dress is black with a black lace around the neck in the pattern of roses. It falls effortlessly to the ground, leaving Jillian standing before Olivia in her black bra, panties, fishnet stockings and high heeled shiny black shoes. Jillian's heart is beating fast and her breath is quick and shallow.

Olivia thinks that there is something so pure about Jillian in the bright sunlight of the morning, which reveals every freckle and contour of Jillian's elegant frame. In the bright light, Olivia is able to appreciate every aspect of Jillian's beauty from her long eyelashes to the golden highlights of her brunette hair curled at the back but raised, revealing the sensuous curve of Jillian's neck.

"Look at me," Olivia says and Jillian raises her gaze from looking at the ground to looking at her boss. Olivia has a mischievous smile on her deep red lips. Jillian is not sure what she sees in Olivia's eyes – is it lust or is it contempt.

"Now the panties," Olivia says waving her finger casually towards Jillian.

Jillian hesitates then moves her hands to the waistband of her panties.

Olivia notices a window cleaner outside the building, cleaning the windows in long strokes of a squeegee and spraying the windows from a bottle. The cleaner seems to be paying no attention to what is happening in the office. Olivia returns her attention to Jillian.

"Slowly, please," Olivia says, studying Jillian's face for a reaction.

Jillian slowly pulls the panties down over her pert bottom.

"Stop for a moment," Olivia says, enjoying the sight of Jillian's cleavage as Jillian is bent towards Olivia and the glimpse of Jillian's tuft of pubic hair.

Jillian looks at Olivia with her beautiful dark eyes.

"Now continue," Olivia says, devouring Jillian with her gaze as Jillian pulls her panties down over her white stockings.

"Give them to me, please," Olivia says with her palm out.

Jillian hands the panties to Olivia who puts them in the top drawer of her desk.

"Now caress yourself for me, between your legs," Olivia says very matter of factly.

Jillian hesitates for a moment then closes her eyes and a hand goes down between her legs.

"Play with yourself. Do it slowly," Olivia says and then her gaze is caught by something outside her office window.

"Put your fingers in deep," Olivia says as a window cleaner starts to clean the windows outside Olivia's office.

Jillian follows Olivia's instructions and her fingers caress her inner folds deeply in a steady rhythm.

"Taste it," Olivia says.

Jillian gingerly puts her fingers from between her legs to her mouth.

"Lick your fingers like a lollipop," Olivia says.

Jillian's tongue licks her fingers in one long lick after another.

Olivia has noticed that the window washer has seen something is going on in the office. The cleaner pretends to be working but keeps stealing glimpses of what is happening in Olivia's office.

"Now remove your bra," Olivia says.

Jillian unhooks her bra from behind and her breasts fall forward.

"Squeeze and pull your nipples," Olivia says.

Jillian pauses for a moment then moves her hand to her breasts and follows Olivia's instruction, squeezing and pulling her nipples, causing her breasts to jiggle and move forward and back, until her nipples are hard little buds.

The window cleaner's eyes look like they are going to pop out of his head. The cleaner is no longer pretending to clean the windows but has his eyes glued to Jillian, enjoying every delicate curve of her.

"Now crawl over here, under my desk," Olivia says and Jillian hangs her head and gets down on all fours to the floor. Jillian crawls over the carpet, her bottom swaying from side to side as she moves under Olivia's desk.

"Now lick my shoes," Olivia says.

Jillian bends down and her pink tongue licks the shiny black leather of Olivia's stiletto. Jillian's bottom is pointed towards the window cleaner and he examines every crevice between her legs.

"I want to see how wet you are, babe," Olivia says, "Remove my shoe and put my big toe inside you."

Jillian removes Olivia's shoe and guides Olivia's foot between her legs and feels Olivia move her foot forward and backwards inside her.

"Now get in close," Olivia says, opening her legs to reveal that she is not wearing any panties.

Jillian leans forward to delicately lick between Olivia's legs, stimulating her clitoris and vagina, until Olivia releases a soft moan.

There is a buzz sound and a light flashes on Olivia's telephone on her desk.

"What is it now?" Olivia complains aloud and then says "Stay there, babe."

There is a man's voice over the intercom, "Olivia, I need to see you straight away."

"Can't it wait, Aaron?" Olivia says, "I'm a bit distracted at the moment."

"No, it can't wait, Olivia. Rosen Bank is going to be moving on the company in the stock market tomorrow," Aaron says.

"OK, come in then," Olivia says as Jillian licks then sucks on Olivia's clitoris.

Olivia straightens her blouse and runs her hand through her hair to neaten it and turns on CNN with a remote control on her desk to cover the sound of Jillian's attentions.

When the door opens, Jillian stops licking.

"Keep going. I'm almost there," Olivia whispers to Jillian.

Aaron walks into the office and does not notice the pile of Jillian's clothes on the floor. He clearly has a head full of steam.

The window cleaner is clearly intrigued and Olivia glowers at him with her eyes widened as if to say, 'What are you looking at?'

"We need to get on the telephone to key shareholders," Aaron says. There is a vein bulging in the side of his neck and Olivia can't help but picture Aaron as an erect penis which brings a slight smile to her face.

"Mm," Olivia says, feeling a wave of pleasure start to peak.

"Are you OK for me to do that?" Aaron asks.

"Mm," Olivia says, closing her eyes for a moment.

"Good, well I'll get onto it now," Aaron says departing the room.

'You do that,' Olivia says breathlessly.

CHAPTER 2. MULTITUDES

Antoinette Ward walks through the MET gallery with Tina Scott, a gorgeous young investment banker, immaculately groomed in a dark grey skirt with a white blouse, intricately patterned stockings and glowing red hair in a raised ponytail, tied with a black ribbon. They have come to the opening of a new exhibition of modern American art sponsored by Antoinette's Rosen Bank.

Antoinette hands Tina a glass of champagne from a handsome waiter's silver tray. Tina gently brushes Antoinette's hand and looks into her blue eyes and smiles.

Antoinette feels like all is right with the world. After a long period of preparation, her company is finally ready to buy a controlling interest in Harrison Savings and Loan. Also after a long period of being single, Antoinette has finally found her princess. She had not even known what she was looking for in a partner until now.

Antoinette thinks about all of the reasons she loves Tina – she is smart, reliable, makes Antoinette's toes curl in bed, and shares the same interests, opera, modern art and sculpture. Tina has also managed to line up all the major shareholders in Harrison Savings and Loan to sell their shares to Rosen Bank tomorrow, allowing Antoinette to settle an old score with her arch rival, Olivia Harrison.

Antoinette and Tina walk around the gallery then stop to admire a large abstract artwork titled 'Interiors' which has many small blocks in multiple colors forming an elaborate swirling pattern.

"I love it," says Tina.

"I love you," says Antoinette.

"Meet me in the bathroom in five," Tina whispers, "I'll be in the second stall from the door."

After Tina leaves for the bathroom, Antoinette approaches Josie James, the owner of the galley, and buys "Interiors" for Tina, a present to celebrate the takeover of Harrison, and another large work entitled

"Multitudes", an intricate painting showing long branches on a beach a night with a bright fire at the top of the interwoven branches.

After the purchase Antoinette goes to the toilets which are down a corridor in the middle of the gallery.

"Hello?" Antoinette says.

"In here Toni," whispers Tina.

Antoinette opens the door to find Tina naked from the waist down and stroking herself with a mischievous grin on her face. Tina's skirt and panties are neatly hanging on a hook on the back of the toilet door.

"Well you are a bad girl," says Antoinette, "That is only mine to play with. Turn around."

Tina follows Antoinette's instruction and bends over with her bottom in the air.

Antoinette admires Tina's shapely behind for a moment before smacking her bottom with an open hand, leaving a red handprint on Tina's pale skin.

"Not bad," Antoinette says looking at the handprint, "But I don't like the lack of symmetry."

Antoinette then slaps Tina's other buttock, leaving another hand print so the two handprints together form a butterfly pattern.

"Much better," says Antoinette, reaching between Tina's legs, "Doesn't take much for you to get aroused."

Tina then faces Antoinette with her eyes aflame with desire and they lock lips while Antoinette runs two fingers gently over Tina's clit with one hand and caresses Tina's breasts over her white blouse with the other hand. Antoinette then removes the ribbon from Tina's hair and it falls upon her shoulders, the sun falling down upon them from the skylight above.

Antoinette curls her hand around the back of Tina's head to pull her close as they kiss for what seems like an eternity, while Antoinette continues to caress and tease Tina's clit until Tina starts to throb with desire and pleasure.

•

CHAPTER 3. HOSTILE TAKEOVER

The next day Olivia starts to appreciate the seriousness of her predicament as the trading figures from the stock market start to come in. Olivia paces the boardroom at Harrison Savings and Loan like Blackbeard preparing his pirate crew to storm a Royal frigate.

Olivia's inner circle all look to the ground rather than the trading figures on the computer screens. They know the game is already over.

"I spoke to the investors yesterday. I thought they were still on board with us," Aaron says.

"Can't we bring in new investors or can I buy more shares?" Olivia says.

"You can't liquidate enough assets quickly enough," Aaron says, "All the pieces on the board have been played."

"It's never too late. OK get out of my office. I have calls to make," Olivia says.

The members of the inner circle leave and Aaron shuts the door very quietly behind him.

Olivia starts making telephone calls to try and sure up her position as chairperson of Harrison Savings and Loan. Some of the major shareholders do not pick up. Others offer excuses. Olivia calls in some favors and has some success in convincing some shareholders not to sell to Rosen Bank. Olivia realises that she is still short of the number of major shareholders to resist the takeover.

Time to bite the bullet, she thinks. Olivia dials the number of Louis Muir, her father's old business partner who she once had an affair with.

"Hello?" Louis answers the telephone, looking out the large window of his study at his country estate.

"Louis, it's me, Olivia."

"What do you want, Olivia?" Louis says, a wry smile on his lips.

"Have you been following the stock market reports?" Olivia asks tapping her fingers on her desk.

"No, what's happened?" Louis lies.

"Has someone from Rosen Bank contacted you?" Olivia asks.

"Well, I don't manage my shares these days. My broker looks after all that and I've told him not to contact me anymore but just use his own discretion," Louis lies again.

"Antoinette Ward wants to take over Harrison Savings and Loan. We can't let that happen," Olivia says, hating the hint of desperation in her voice.

"Drive over here Olivia and we can discuss it," Louis says.

"What now?" Olivia asks.

"When did you want to discuss it then?"

"OK, I'm coming over. See you after six," Olivia says.

"Goodbye Olivia," Louis says, sitting back and enjoying the new painting on the wall of his study which is called "Multitudes".

CHAPTER 4. THE GIFT

Antoinette sits in the darkness in her office sipping whisky from a crystal glass while looking over the financials of the takeover of Harrison Savings and Loan on her laptop. *We are almost there*, she thinks.

Tina knocks then enters the office in her red sequined dress glittering by the light of the stars and city lights outside the office window.

Tina puts a finger to her lips and smiles. Tina then lets her dress drop from her shoulders and it falls to the floor.

Antoinette momentarily holds her breath at Tina's beautiful silhouette, black lingerie, black stockings and shiny black high heeled stilettos.

Tina walks closer to Antoinette with a mischievous smile then leans forward to kiss her.

"Thank you for the present," Tina says.

"My pleasure," Antoinette says.

Antoinette interlocks her hands behind Tina's neck and draws Tina to her until their lips are almost touching. Antoinette strains to reach her lips, her silky hair falling upon Antoinette's face, Tina giggles then kisses Antoinette.

Tina then sits on Antoinette's lap and Antoinette runs her hand over Tina's silky stockings and then to the bare skin above the stockings. Antoinette feels her heart quicken as the blood surges through her, making her light-headed with passion.

Tina removes Antoinette's jacket and then folds it neatly on the desk. She then unbuttons Antoinette's shirt and kisses Antoinette's neck then chest above each open button in a thoroughly attentive way. Tina's attention to detail is another thing Antoinette loves about her. Tina gently runs her hands through Antoinette's hair. Tina's breath is hot and sweet upon Antoinette.

Tina then looks into Antoinette's eyes, deeply and they kiss. Antoinette and Tina feel totally connected and everything else just fades into the background. They communicate through soft lips and gentle touch.

CHAPTER 5. THE ESTATE

Olivia asks her driver to remain in the car on the pebble driveway of the estate of Louis Muir. His Georgian style mansion towers over them. Olivia is surprised when Louis opens the large door to his house himself. Louis has aged considerably since she last saw him which was before his wife left him, probably after she found out about what was going on between Olivia and Louis.

"Come in Olivia," Louis gestures for Olivia to go inside with a smile.

There is a fire crackling in the front lounge room of the mansion. There is a crystal glass decanter with whiskey and two crystal glasses next to it. Next to the decanter there is a small black box wrapped in black ribbon.

"I was just having a quiet drink to celebrate your visit. Would you care to join me?" Louis says, not even waiting for Olivia to answer but pouring her a glass regardless.

"Thank you," Olivia says receiving the glass and drinking it down in one gulp, the whiskey burning all the way down.

Louis smiles again and asks, "A hard day?"

"It's been a great day," Olivia says staring into the fire.

"The nature of business and life is we rise, we fall, and we build again. Life is so much easier when you realise that," Louis says sitting on the leather chesterfield couch opposite Olivia.

"It's not over yet. Do I have your support?" Olivia asks looking at Louis, trying to read his expression. His eyes close.

"Louis?" Olivia says.

"You know I miss seeing you. I found it very hard when my wife left me and you refused to see me anymore. To be honest, I felt betrayed," Louis says.

"We could not go on seeing each other. You know me. I can't sit still for too long. I regret Isla leaving you. I'm sorry but that was beyond my control," Olivia says.

"Well I would like to *see* you again one more time," Louis says opening his eyes then pouring two more whiskeys for them.

"I'm right before you," Olivia says.

"You know what I mean. In the flesh, so to speak," Louis says, staring into Olivia's eyes.

Olivia pauses for a moment to think. Louis casts his eyes over Olivia from top to bottom, savouring this moment.

Olivia says "What do you have in mind?"

"I just want to see you one more time, Olivia," Louis says with a sad smile, "I often think about you."

Olivia looks into Louis's eyes. There is a mixture of sadness and determination.

"I have a small gift for you in the box next to the decanter," Louis says.

Olivia leans forward to pick up the box, removes the ribbon and opens the lid. There is a thin gold chain on black satin.

Olivia looks at Louis who smiles in encouragement. Olivia pulls the chain out and it drops from her hand onto the floor. She then pulls out the black satin and realises it is a blindfold. There is also a small piece of paper.

Dearest Olivia, if we will only have this one more night together then I want to remember it well. I seek that you grant me one wish which is that you place this blindfold on, disrobe then place the gold chain around your neck and let me take you for a walk. Yours now and forever, Louis.

Olivia cannot quite believe that Louis has written this note. She reads it again. *What is the harm?* Olivia thinks to herself.

Olivia takes off her jacket and folds it over the chair. She then holds the blindfold up to her eyes and ties it behind the back of her head. It is silky soft.

Louis sits back and sips upon his whiskey and lights a Cuban cigar, one he had been saving for a special occasion.

Olivia unbuttons her white blouse, revealing a lacy white bra and soft smooth skin.

Olivia stands up and lets the blouse float to the floor. She then unhooks her bra, releasing her breasts which glow in the light of the open fire.

Louis swallows awkwardly as he gazes upon Olivia's statuesque beauty. He steps towards her and gently runs his fingers down the side of her face, along her neck and then down over one breast then along her stomach.

Louis studies Olivia as if he is looking at the work of a master sculptor, cupping her breasts and running his thumbs over her nipples until they start to harden, pointing upwards.

"You are incredible," Louis whispers in Olivia's ear, "Please remove your skirt as well."

Olivia unzips her skirt from the side and allows it to drop to the floor. Olivia is wearing black panties, a black garter belt, black stockings and stilettos.

Louis caresses Olivia's bottom and kisses her along the neck then brushes the back of his hand along the top of her thighs above her black stockings.

"You can keep the rest on, Olivia," Louis says quietly in almost a whisper, "Now please put the chain on. It's by your feet."

Olivia bends down to try and find the chain on the rug. Louis almost sighs at the sight of Olivia bending down. There is something almost impossibly beautiful about the sight of Olivia searching for the gold chain. Olivia's hands pat the rug until she finds the thin chain and hooks it around her neck so that the chain falls between her breasts onto the floor.

Louis walks behind Olivia and reaches between Olivia's legs and picks the end of the chain up and brings the chain up so that it lightly touches Olivia's black panties. Louis sits on the coffee table behind Olivia and gently moves the chain from one side to the others, brushing it from side to side.

Louis then goes in front of Olivia and softly kisses her lips. Olivia is very still like a statue. Louis holds the chain and gently tugs upon it.

"Come forward Olivia," Louis says watching Olivia's body slowly sway as she walks on her stilettos across the lounge room, guiding her around the furniture.

Olivia keeps her head very straight as Louis walks her through the mansion and then opens the French doors to the side courtyard with Olivia feeling an immediate chill.

It is cold but Olivia does not flinch as they walk into the courtyard, the wind cold on Olivia's skin.

Louis switches a flood light on in the courtyard. Louis moves behind Olivia and passes the gold chain between her legs and then grabs it on the other side. He brushes his hand over one of Olivia's buttocks. He can feel her shivering.

"You're cold," Louis says, "I'll start a fire."

Louis lights some wood in an ornate cast iron fire pit in the center of the courtyard.

When the fire is burning brightly, Louis asks, "Is that better, Olivia?"

Olivia nods her head.

"Now Olivia, please remove your panties," Louis asks.

Olivia pauses for a moment. *I have come this far*, she thinks. *Why not go further?*

Olivia slips her black panties down her muscular thighs and shapely legs, down over her stilettos.

"Hand them to me please, Olivia," Louis says.

Olivia does as instructed and Louis immediately throws them onto the fire pit.

"Please bend over and reach for your ankles," Louis whispers into Olivia's ear.

Olivia follows Louis's instruction and reaches her hands down her legs until she is bent over and holding onto her ankles.

The wind blows through the surrounding pines making a mysterious noise.

Louis then moves closer making sure not to obscure the light to examine every crevice and fold of Olivia.

Louis uses the gold chain to gently pull back Olivia's outer lips to see the pink flesh underneath. He runs a finger between Olivia's legs and notices a slight glisten on his finger.

"Nicely wet," Louis says, "Well done Olivia."

Olivia quietly seethes underneath the blindfold, wanting to rip it off and stomp on Louis's foot with her stiletto.

Olivia pictures this image in her mind as Louis reaches his hands around Olivia to caress her breasts. He holds each breast and gently squeezes each breast and lightly strokes each nipple. Olivia is silent.

Louis's butler, Sean Hughes, sits silently in the courtyard watching from a deckchair. The butler is lean and handsome with a chiselled physique. Having worked for Louis for the last five years, nothing surprises him and he is more than happy to assist his boss with some of his more unusual requests.

Louis beckons Sean to come forward. Sean lifts unzips his trousers and is almost painfully erect underneath.

Olivia hears someone walking towards her.

"Who's there?" Olivia asks.

"Open your legs a bit more, Olivia," Louis says, "I have asked my butler to penetrate you. It's OK, he is wearing a condom."

"Are you mad, Louis?" Olivia says.

"Quiet, my dear," says Louis.

Louis rubs his finger back and forth between Olivia's legs, so that her body sways back and forth a little. Sean gently traces his fingers up and down Olivia's back and then along the side of her legs.

Olivia moves her legs further apart.

"Olivia, can you please pull your lips apart for me," Louis whispers into Olivia's ear.

Olivia opens her mouth.

"Sorry Olivia, I meant down here," Louis says moving his fingers back and forth between Olivia's legs until Olivia moves her hand under her legs and moves the lips of her vagina apart with two fingers.

Louis bends down to look between Olivia's legs.

"Just as I remembered it, perfect in every way," Louis says then kisses the back of Olivia's neck with small kisses down her spine.

Sean moves forward and presses top of his penis into Olivia, letting the tip stimulate Olivia's clitoris, then slowly working it deeper into Olivia.

Olivia moans as the butler pushes even deeper and moves backwards and forwards into Olivia while Louis kisses her neck and back and fondles her breasts and thighs.

Olivia's breath becomes quick and shallow while the Sean slowly moves back and forwards. Sean quickens the pace of his thrusting and Olivia starts to pant.

Louis whispers into Olivia's ears, "You are on fire."

Sean has to stifle a moan as he climaxes then slowly backs away into the darkness.

Olivia is heaving in ecstasy. Louis moves his fingers between Olivia's legs.

"You are so wet," Louis whispers into Olivia's ear.

"You may remove the blindfold, Olivia," Louis says.

Olivia stands up and turns around and removes the blindfold to see Louis smiling at her.

•

CHAPTER 6. SWEETER THAN CANDY

Olivia feels quietly satisfied as she sits in the back seat of her limousine knowing that one major shareholder will not be selling his sizeable portion of Harrison shares to Antoinette Ward.

Time for a little rest and recreation, Olivia thinks before telephoning Candice.

"Candy, it's me, Olivia. I need you. Can you meet me at the club?"

"I can't really get away right now, Olivia," Candice says in a whisper, "Aaron is here. We were just about to – you know, make love."

"Candy, can you do this for me – I'll call back on skype and if you can put the skype on your telephone and let me watch – that will entertain me on the drive back to New York. I want you to give Aaron the blowjob of his life and make him come onto your breasts. Then I'll call you and you need to leave saying it's an emergency – you have a major client who is in crisis. Then after that, I want you to just put a coat over yourself and those high heeled shoes I like and catch a taxi to the club. Do you understand that, Candy?"

"Yes, Olivia," Candice says disconnecting the call as Aaron enters the bedroom on his way to the en-suite.

"Who was that?" Aaron asks.

"Oh, just the office. They have a problem with a client who is in crisis. They think they can handle it but will call me if it gets out of hand," Candice says.

"I hope they can handle it. I've been looking forward to *date night* all week," Aaron says as he closes the door to the en-suite.

Candice dials Olivia's skype number and sees Olivia in the back of her limousine.

"OK?" Candice whispers into the telephone.

"Can you prop your phone on the bookcase so I can see your bed? Put a jumper on the phone to hide it?" Olivia says.

"Sure," Candice says.

When Aaron re-enters the room he is totally naked and his bare bottom fills the screen on Olivia's telephone. *Not bad*, Olivia thinks. *He must be working out.*

Olivia can then see Candice upon the bed. Candice pulls her nightie over her head and crawls over the bed to Aaron and starts to kiss his chest and lick his nipples then kisses along his neck and then his mouth.

Olivia is impressed with the size of Aaron's erection. It seems bigger than she remembers him. *Perhaps it is something to do with perspective –* she thinks. Candice gets down in front of Aaron and she licks along the shaft of Aaron's penis. Candice then encircles the tip of his penis with her mouth and moves her mouth forwards and backwards while sucking it. Candice then lifts up and removes her nightie and moves her chest forward so that her bare breasts surround Aaron's penis and she pushes them around the penis and then moves up and down.

Aaron and Candice kiss each other passionately. Olivia feels almost jealous of them and starts to miss her girlfriend who is now jet-setting around Europe for the spring fashion shows.

Aaron has an intense look on his face as Candice returns to sucking the tip of his shaft. She then sucks his testicles while pumping Aaron's erection with one hand and stroking herself with her other hand.

"Good girl," Olivia says to herself, impressed with Candice's techniques.

Candice then caresses herself with one hand while bobbing up and down upon Aaron's erection until he looks like he is going to come.

Olivia presses Candice's number on the contacts on her telephone.

Candice works harder on Aaron's erection, trying to ignore the ringing phone under her jumper on the bookcase. Aaron is so much on the verge he hardly notices the noise of the ringing phone.

Aaron moans as Candice uses her hand to pump Aaron's erection as it sprays hot sperm upon her breasts.

"Sorry Aaron, the phone's ringing," Candice excuses herself and goes over to the bookcase.

Aaron lies upon the bed with his eyes closed, savouring the lingering feeling of release.

"Hello?" Candice answers the mobile.

"That was a very impressive performance. It made me forget my troubles for a little while," Olivia says.

"Mm," Candice says.

"But it made me want you even more. I'm so hungry for you," Olivia says.

"Yes," Candice says.

"OK, I'll see you down the club," Olivia says.

"OK, I'll be there as soon as I can," Candice says. She then turns to Aaron and says, "Sorry darling, they need me desperately down at the office. One of our clients is in crisis."

"What?" Aaron does not understand.

Candice sits on the bed next to Aaron and says, "Aaron, honey. The office needs me to come down there for a short while."

"Can't it wait until tomorrow morning?" Aaron says.

"No, well the nature of business these days is that it operates 24 hours per day. It will be too late to deal with the problem in the morning," Candice says rubbing Aaron's back.

"OK then well I'm coming with you," Aaron says.

"No, that's OK. I'll just catch a cab. I'll take it straight from our building," Candice says.

"Well, OK but on one condition," Aaron says.

"What's that?"

"Well, because date night has been cut short we need to have another date night tomorrow night," Aaron says.

"Well OK, then but I would like to try something new tomorrow but I'll tell you about it then," Candice says, kissing Aaron on the lips while patting his butt.

Aaron seems to be drifting to sleep as Candice pulls her long coat from her cupboard and grabs her white high heeled shoes and her purse.

When she is in the lounge room she puts the coat onto her naked body and buttons it up and pulls on her high heeled shoes. She then quickly brushes her hair and puts on red lipstick in the lounge room mirror then smooths it with her finger.

Candice waves down a taxi and drives downtown to Olivia's club. The bouncer remains impassive as she passes past him into the club.

A group of young business women are laughing, playing a drinking game at the bar, taking turns at downing shots every time a beautiful stripper on stage removes an item of clothing. When the stripper is down to the merest of bikinis, she climbs into an oversized champagne glass and writhes in the glass as an assistant pours champagne upon her. The stripper then spins on her bottom around in the glass and kicks the champagne out into the women in the crowd. At the end of the performance an assistant hands the performer a towel as she leaves the glass and the crowd claps.

Candice searches for Olivia amongst the women at the club and eventually finds her there alone in her office at the back, with a glass of champagne ready for her.

"Candy, you have kept me waiting," Olivia says sternly.

"I came as fast as I could," Candice says.

"Well you are going to have to make it up to me," Olivia says.

"Yes?"

"Lose the coat," Olivia directs.

Candice unbuttons her coat to reveal her naked body.

Olivia comes in close and touches the almost dry sperm upon Candice's breasts.

"Disgusting," Olivia says holding her finger up for Candice to see.

"You told me to come..." Candice starts but Olivia puts her finger to Candice's lips.

"Ssh, Candy. Too much talk already. I have had a day you would not believe and I need some ... well, peace of mind," Olivia says, "There is a shower through that door over there. Wash up and I'll join you in there in a minute."

Candice walks in her high white heels to the bathroom, Olivia enjoying every step. Olivia listens to the shower going as she enjoys another swig from the champagne bottle. Olivia then removes her own clothes and folds them over the chair. When she opens the door to the bathroom there is steam everywhere and Candice is naked and wet in the shower, soaping her thigh and looking directly at Olivia with a hungry look.

Olivia joins Candice in the shower and they hug each other while Olivia kisses Candice with a mouth so wide it seems like Olivia wants to devour her.

"You know what to do," Olivia says and Candice drops to her knees in the shower and starts to caress Olivia between her legs with her tongue in a slow and sensuous movement while reaching up and stimulating Olivia's nipples with her hands. Olivia grinds her vagina into Candice's face which seems to excite Candice even more as her attentions to Olivia become more urgent and intense.

"You are such a hot, little minx," Olivia says as she feels her body start to be overtaken by pleasure, "Keep going, Candy. I'm almost there."

Candice sucks upon Olivia's delicate clit, making Olivia weak at the knees with pleasure. Olivia releases a long moan as she climaxes and Candice looks up smiling, pleased with her handiwork.

Olivia leaves the shower and dries herself with a towel and puts on a bathrobe. Candice does the same and they sit in the bathroom amongst the steam.

"Now Candy. I know you have been doing all the work tonight to bring other people pleasure. I realise you should have some pleasure too but to be honest I'm too selfish to give anyone any pleasure tonight. That's why I've asked my secretary to come to the club. She's stripping for the first time and I've asked her to join us afterwards for some fun," Olivia says.

"But I want you, Olivia," Candice says.

"Well you have just had me and that's all I have to give I'm afraid. Dry your hair and put on that dress on the hanger on the back of the door. I'll get changed in the office."

After Olivia has left, Candice opens the bathroom cabinet drawer and finds a hair dryer. She blow-dries her hair then examines the dress hanging on the back of the bathroom door.

It is a soft blue velvet dress that Candice is surprised to find hugs her curves perfectly – almost too perfectly as the full shape and contours of her nipples can clearly be seen through the soft fabric of the dress. Candice then puts on her high white heels.

Olivia is dressed in a sleek black designer dress, black stockings, and black stilettos.

"That dress is perfect on you," Olivia says, running her hands over the soft fabric of her dress then pinching Candice's nipples until they are hard and pointy against the blue velvet.

"Perfect," Olivia says, "Now hurry we don't want to miss Jillian on her debut."

Olivia and Candice hold hands and walk to a table at the front of the stage reserved for Olivia.

"Now ladies, we have a very special treat for you – a little number called *The Secretary*," the DJ announces as Olivia's secretary Jillian enters the stage looking somewhat nervous and the crowd claps politely.

The sound of typing along with electronic music can be heard and Jillian takes a seat on a black chair on stage and pretends to type. She is wearing high black heels, sheer stockings, a tight check skirt, a white blouse with generous décolletage. Her long hair is rolled up into two French plaits.

Jillian then pretends to answer the telephone and smiles and flirts with the imaginary person on the other end of the telephone. Jillian plays with her hair and turns one foot around and around until her shoe becomes loose and falls to the ground.

Jillian then unbuttons her blouse and pulls her bra upwards and moves her hands over her breasts in a circular motion in time with the music. Jillian then sticks two fingers deeply into her mouth and licks them on the way out and she then applies the wet hand to each of her nipples in turn.

Jillian then stands up and reaches under her skirt and pulls down her white panties and tosses them to one side then bends over so that the cheeks of her bottom peak from under her short check skirt.

Jillian then sits on the chair facing the audience and licks her fingers again and proceeds to rub between her legs in front of the audience, a look of sensuous pleasure upon her face.

Jillian then raises her legs high up while still stroking herself between the legs. Jillian then turns around and grips the chair with one hand and flips her skirt up with the other hand and then moves her fingers in and out of her vagina from behind until her vagina glistens. Jillian looks behind to the audience who are transfixed by her wanton display.

At the end of the performance, the crowd claps enthusiastically. Olivia and Candice return to the office. Olivia claps as Jillian enters the office.

"That was amazing Jillian, well done," Olivia says.

"Thank you, Olivia. I'm glad you liked it. I did my best," Jillian says.

"You sure did. Jillian, this is Candy," Olivia introduces the two of them and they shake hands.

"We've met before," Jillian says and Candice just smiles.

"Now Jillian, Candy I have something I want you to wear," Olivia says as she hands each woman a small bundle of black clothing.

Each woman examines the bundle – black thigh high tights and a black mask with cat's ears.

"Put these on first and then I will explain the task," Olivia says.

Candice unzips the blue velvet dress so that she is naked again and then pulls on the tights and secures the cat's mask onto her head. Jillian does the same.

"Now I want you to get to know each other. You are both cats on heat and you are irresistible to each other. You want to explore each other with your tongues," Olivia says, "Now get down on the floor and crawl around."

The two women gingerly get down onto the floor and crawl around on all fours, their bottoms swaying as they crawl.

"Now Candy, you lie on your back with your legs apart. Yes, that's right. Good girl," Olivia says encouraging Candice.

"Jillian you start to lick between Candy's legs with long cat licks like you are licking up milk from a plate," Olivia says and soon Jillian has her bottom up in the air and her tongue lapping at Candice's vagina.

"Now Jillian, you position your vagina over Candy's mouth so you can both lick each other like cats. That's it," Olivia says as both of the women assume the sixty-nine position and lick each other's vaginas with long licks and make soft moans of pleasure like cats purring.

Olivia then goes to the bar fridge in the office and takes out a container of milk.

"Now Candy, you sit up for a moment. Up here upon the desk," Olivia says and Candice perches herself on the edge of the desk.

"Legs apart please," Olivia says, "And open your mouth and stick out your tongue."

Candice spreads her legs apart and sticks out her tongue and Olivia pours milk from the carton onto Candice's open mouth and it pours down over her breasts and between her legs.

"Now Jillian. Could you please clean up this mess?" Olivia asks Jillian who immediately locks her mouth with Candice's mouth and their tongues intertwine. Then Jillian kisses along Candice's neck then licks the milk from Candice's breasts, the flat of her tongue passing over

Candice's nipples then Jillian continued downward, kissing and licking Candice's stomach and then further down between Candice's legs then down her legs.

"And the floor please Jillian," Olivia says as Jillian continues to lick the small puddle of milk from the floor of the office.

"Now how do we show affection, Jillian – as a cat I mean?" Olivia asks and Jillian rubs herself against Olivia and then Candice.

"Jillian, I think Candy still has some milk on her but it is deep inside. Can you reach it with your tongue?"

Jillian kneels on the floor and starts to kiss and suck upon Candice's vagina. Jillian patiently laps Candice's clitoris in a slow and steady motion until Candice starts to moan with pleasure. When the pleasure has subsided, Olivia claps her hands.

"You are the most beautiful pets I could ever hope for. I feel like I can take on the world again with you two by my side," Olivia says.

•

CHAPTER 7. BLACK PEARL

Olivia looks at the crowd of shareholders gathered at the extraordinary general meeting of Harrison Savings and Loan and sees Louis chatting with the other major shareholders to one side. Olivia catches his eye and he gestures with his head to one side and starts moving to one of the side doors and leaves the door. Olivia moves down from the stage and follows him out the door. A number of shareholders watch her as she walks towards the door. Olivia looks stunning. She is wearing a tight fitting houndstooth skirt with black stockings and black high heels. Olivia's hair is up in a French roll, displaying her slender neck. Olivia's lips are deep rouge and she wears a string of black pearls.

Louis continues to walk down the hallway without looking at Olivia but he knows she is following him. He walks into Olivia's office and sits down on her black leather executive office chair.

"Your panties please, Olivia," says Louis.

"What? Are you crazy, Louis? I'm speaking in five minutes. I thought you had something to tell me," Olivia says, trying to suppress the hint of panic in her voice.

"Panties, Olivia. On the desk, please," Louis says watching for Olivia's reaction.

Olivia unzips her houndstooth skirt and steps out of it then pulls down her black lace panties and places them on her mahogany desk.

"Legs apart Olivia," Louis says, gesturing with his hand. Olivia spreads her legs slightly.

"A bit wider please," Louis says, studying Olivia's face.

"I have to get back to the shareholder meeting," Olivia says harshly.

"Hush now. You can go back to the meeting when those pearls around your neck glisten," Louis says with a wry smile.

"What do you mean, Louis? I don't have time for your games," Olivia says.

"Firstly unhook your pearls from around your neck and string them between your legs then ride them like you were riding a horse," Louis says.

"You have to be joking," Olivia says indignantly.

"The sooner you start, the sooner you can go back to your meeting," Louis says, trying to hide a smirk from his face, relishing every moment.

"Do you want me to help you unhook the pearls?" asks Louis.

Olivia nods and Louis unhooks the black pearls at the back. He then runs his hands over Olivia's pert buttocks then grabs one buttock and pulls it to one side to look between Olivia's legs.

"You have the most beautiful vagina," Louis says, "Now get to work."

Louis hands Olivia the string of black pearls and Louis returns to the black office chair.

Olivia strings the pearls between her legs and starts to move them between her legs.

"Grind into them," Louis says.

Olivia starts to move her hips forward and back, grinding herself into the string of pearls. Olivia looks so delicious to Louis that he can feel himself starting to salivate and can also feel his erection straining against his suit trousers.

Olivia's mobile starts to buzz.

"Don't stop," Louis says while the mobile continues to buzz.

Olivia starts to grind into the pearls more wantonly, her hips now moving up sharply, her eyes closed and her breath quick and quiet.

"Show me the pearls," Louis commands.

Olivia opens her eyes and holds the pearls up with one hand. The pearls sparkle and glisten.

"OK. You're done. Now get dressed, you have a meeting to address," Louis says, leaving the room abruptly without closing the door, with Jillian and the other staff stealing a glimpse of Olivia getting dressed then quickly going about their duties as Olivia leaves her office in a rush to get to the meeting on time.

"Where were you?" says Aaron in a whisper as Olivia joins him on the stage, "I tried to call you. The shareholders are getting restless."

"Never mind," Olivia says.

Olivia walks to the lectern and speaks to the shareholders about the rebranding of the company and goes over all the positive developments that have occurred under the present Board of Management and explains her future vision for Harrison, a company that was originally established by her family over one hundred years ago. Olivia's eyes scan the crowd to try and get a sense of the mood of the room but her eyes keep going back to Louis who is seated again with the other major shareholders. *He still has that smirk on his face*, Olivia thinks.

Aaron follows Olivia and goes over all the financial data of Harrison with the shareholders. He is followed by Antoinette Ward who gives a very charismatic talk about increasing shareholder value and returns through Harrison being part of a much bigger financial group. Olivia sits at a table on the side of the stage. She looks over at Louis who winks at Olivia and blows her a kiss.

Aaron announces a vote will be taken by a show of hands as to who will support the takeover. Louis raises his hand with a broad smile on his face. The other major shareholders look at Louis and then hesitate for a moment looking awkwardly at Olivia or the ground then raise their hands in support of the takeover. This is followed by the majority of the smaller shareholders.

"Let the minutes record that the takeover of Harrison by Rosen Bank is approved," Aaron announces, sounding exasperated. There is a smattering of applause in the room. Olivia's cheeks burn red and for the first time in years she feels like she could cry but no tears come, just a terrible sinking feeling, like she is melting into the floor as Antoinette Ward is appointed the new chairperson of the Board of Directors of Harrison Savings and Loan. As Olivia leaves the room, followed by Aaron and her inner circle, she glimpses Antoinette shaking hands with Louis and the other major shareholders.

At the lift Olivia turns to her staff and says, "I want to be left alone."

Olivia takes the lift straight to the basement of the building and enters her limousine determined to obliterate this day from her mind. The limousine takes off at great speed and Olivia drinks whiskey from a silver flask as she travels to her country residence, determined to disappear for a while and plan her revenge.

CHAPTER 8. THE BOX

Jillian is reorganising the filing cabinet when she hears her telephone chiming from her handbag. Jillian rushes over and answers the telephone, "Hello?"

"Jillian, it's me," Olivia says, "What has been happening since I've been away?" says Olivia.

"They've been going through all the data," Jillian whispers into her telephone, as Antoinette is with Tina in the adjoining office.

"What are they up to?" Olivia says.

Jillian takes her phone with her to the toilets, "I don't know. I do know I miss you though."

"I miss you too. Can you get away from the office to spend some time with me and update me with what's happing at Harrison?" Olivia says, looking over the green lawns of her country mansion.

"Yes, I can," Jillian says.

"I'll send my car around to collect you at 6.30pm from your house," Olivia says, "Wear something sexy. I need cheering up."

"Yes," Jillian says.

"Can you shave for me as well?" Olivia says.

"Yes, I will," Jillian says, looking around the toilets to make sure no one is listening to them.

"And bring two vibrators," Olivia requests.

Jillian makes some excuse to Human Resources that she has a sick sister who she needs to support over the next few days.

At 6.30pm Olivia's car is waiting to collect her out the front of Jillian's apartment block. When Jillian is in the backseat of the car, a video screen in the car turns on and Olivia is there, a whiskey in one hand, a cigar in the other.

"Hello Jillian," Olivia says. There are dark rings around her eyes as if she has not been sleeping.

"Hello Olivia," Jillian says.

"Did you shave?" Olivia asks then takes a sip from her drink.

Jillian smiles awkwardly and shyly says, "Yes."

"Let me see," Olivia says.

Jillian looks up at the driver but he has his eyes glued to the road.

Jillian then lifts up her skirt and removes her white panties and pulls them down her legs and over her high heels. Jillian then lifts her skirt to the screen to display her hairless pubic area.

"Beautiful," says Olivia.

"Thank you," Jillian giggles.

"Stroke yourself," Olivia requests.

Jillian looks out the window. She is wearing a prim and pressed white blouse. Her fingers snake to her naked crotch as the limousine speeds through the city on the way to Olivia's country mansion.

"Jillian, show me what you have in your handbag," Olivia directs.

"I bought what you told me to buy, Olivia," Jillian batts her long eyelashes as she opens her handbag to reveal two small vibrators.

"OK, now suck on your fingers Jillian and then lubricate your rear for me," Olivia says in a matter of fact way.

Jillian sucks deeply on her fingers and then licks them in one long lick after another then sits up and slips her finger behind her to explore behind.

Just then a truck driver drives by and honks his horn when next to Olivia's car.

"Jillian, don't get those truck drivers too excited," Olivia says, "Now grab the first vibrator, switch it on and put that into your rear. Now grab the other vibrator and put that in your vagina," Olivia says.

Jillian follows Olivia's instructions so that both vibrators are soon whirring inside her, giving her intense feelings of both shame and pleasure.

"Now sit back and enjoy the ride," Olivia says puffing on her cigar, watching the intensity of Jillian's expressions.

Olivia leaves Jillian like this until Jillian is writhing in the seat in orgasm, gently bucking her hips forward then lightly shaking as she comes.

Olivia studies the look of pleasure on Jillian's face and is almost jealous of Jillian's sweet agony. *Jillian, sweet Jillian*, Olivia thinks and then wonders how Jillian will react to what she has in mind for her.

The Emporia Club women sit with Olivia at her country mansion watching Jillian on the big screen while a scantily clad waiter and waitress serve drinks and cigars to the guests.

When the limousine arrives at the mansion, cameras at the mansion cover Jillian's arrival.

"She's here," Olivia says to the other women.

A French maid wearing nothing but a frilly apron and hat welcomes Jillian to the house and escorts Jillian to her room.

The room is elaborately decorated with a four poster bed in the center of the room. On the bed is a black box with a black ribbon on it.

There is a letter in Olivia's handwriting inside along with other items.

Dearest Jillian,

If you continue to read this letter beyond this point then it will be acceptance of the contract.

From this moment until you leave you hereby agree to be the personal secretary to the Emporia Club.

I want you to go to the wardrobe in your room and put on the outfit that is in the walk in robe then go straight to the meeting room. There will be a name plate for you at the table, an envelope and a small present wrapped in black ribbon. Please open the envelope and follow the instructions inside.

O

•

CHAPTER 9. INNER CIRCLE

Jillian walks into the walk in robe area. There is only one set of clothes in there with a number of items on the one hanger – a sheer black bra, matching panties, black stockings, black suspenders, a black blouse with a red embroidered rose pattern and a short sheer shirt.

On the floor of the robe is a pair of impossibly high shiny black stilettos. Jillian changes into the clothes, puts on the heels, ties her hair up, reapplies her makeup and walks to the meeting room.

The five women who are the inner circle of the Emporia Club are seated around the large oak table in the meeting roam.

The women stop their conversation and turn to look at Jillian as she enters the room, her high heeled shoes click-clacking across the wooden floor.

Olivia is seated amongst them and nods in the direction of the vacant chair. There is a name plate on the table. Jillian sits down and reads the nameplate. It simply says *Secretary*.

As Olivia indicated there is an envelope on the table which also has *Secretary* written on it.

The inner circle is quiet and simply watches Jillian as she reads the note.

Dear Secretary,

Thank you for accepting this position of being Secretary of the Emporia Club.

It is a position of great care and responsibility. You will need to work to the satisfaction of each of the executives of the Emporia Club Board of Management – Bridget, Marion, Annika, Miranda, and Olivia.

Each of the executives has allocated you a task. If you achieve the task allocated you may progress to the next task.

If you fail to complete the task to the satisfaction of the executive then you will experience the consequences set by that executive.

If you successfully achieve all five of the allocated tasks then you will have the pleasure of continuing as the secretary of the Emporia Club.

Your first work task has been allocated by Bridget. You are to perform an erotic striptease in the meeting room following Bridget's instructions commencing when Bridget starts the music.

The Board of Management

Jillian looks around the table at the women around the table. They are well dressed business women and professionals. Two maids and a butler serve the women, wearing nothing more than white aprons.

The woman who Jillian takes to be Bridget lifts her hand and presses a remote control to start music playing. It is an exotic Middle Eastern song with a slow, sensuous electronic pulse.

"Secretary, please dance to the music for us," Bridget says, a soft smile on her face.

Jillian gets up from the chair and moves her arms in time with the music and sways her hips.

"Move more slowly please," Bridget says.

Jillian slows down her movement. The short skirt rides up her body as she dances.

Ringlets of her hair fall upon her back.

Jillian closes her eyes.

"Now remove your blouse and caress your breasts but do it very slowly," Bridget says.

Jillian takes off her black blouse exposing the black sheer bra.

Jillian uses both hands to caress her breasts, pushing them together so that her pointy nipples press against the thin material.

"Pay special attention to your nipples. Please play with them," Bridget requests.

Jillian immediately starts to run her hands over her nipples and strokes and pulls upon them until they are erect and straining against the black, sheer fabric of the bra.

"Now remove your skirt and hand it to me," Bridget says and Jillian removes the skirt, folds it, walks over to Bridget and hands it to her.

Jillian's long legs seem to go on forever in the long black stockings and high heeled shoes.

"Now walk over to the door and stimulate yourself on the door knob," Bridget says.

Every pair of eyes in the room is on Jillian's long legs as she walks over to the door which has a circular polished brass doorknob.

Jillian faces the door and slightly elevates herself forward on her toes to bring her crotch in line with the door nob and moves her vagina back and forward over the knob in time with the music, her bottom facing the Board of Directors.

"Now do the same facing us," Bridget commands.

Jillian turns around and bends over and backs over the door knob and starts to move back and forward over the knob while her breasts swing back and forward against the black sheer material of her bra. Her eyes are closed again.

"Please smile while you do that and open your eyes and look at us," Bridget requests.

Jillian opens her eyes and surveys the table, smiling at each woman with a flash of bright teeth framed by perfect red lips.

"Are you enjoying that?" Bridget asks.

Jillian simply nods her head.

"Now come over here and sit astride my legs," Bridget says as Jillian gets down off the door knob and walks over to Bridget who has pulled her chair back from the boardroom table.

Bridget is wearing grey tailored slacks, a business shirt, and a gold silk tie. She has short blond hair. She taps her thigh as Jillian approaches and straddles Bridget's legs.

"Now rub your pussy against my legs," Bridget requests.

Jillian follows the instruction and grinds herself against Bridget's legs, moving back and forth.

"Play with your nipples again while you do that," Bridget adds.

Jillian's fingers twist and pull upon her nipples again as her crotch continues to grind into Bridget's leg.

Next Bridget moves her hand to where Jillian is grinding and feels between Jillian's legs and Jillian grinds into Bridget's hand.

"Lick my fingers," Bridget says holding her hand up to Jillian's mouth.

Jillian licks each finger while continuing to grind into Bridget's leg.

"Suck my fingers," Bridget commands and Jillian moves her mouth over Bridget's fingers and moves her mouth back and forward over them, leaving a shiny trail of saliva between her mouth and Bridget's hand.

"Now step backwards and turn around and slowly remove your panties with both hands and then stay bent over," Bridget says.

Once Jillian is bent over, Bridget studies each curve and crevice of Jillian's behind. Bridget cannot resist touching the smooth skin of Jillian's buttocks and then gives each buttock a light pinch.

"Well done Jillian, you have achieved your first performance target," Bridget says and the Board of Management applaud.

CHAPTER 10. EN PLEIN AIR

Jillian returns to the meeting table and sits bare bottomed upon the chair facing the Board of Directors.

"Jillian your next challenge has been allocated by me," says Marion, a curly haired woman in her forties with a French accent.

"You will accompany me in Olivia's car. Olivia's chauffeur will drive us to the *Lookout*, a certain location in the hills known for lovers to park their cars and do what comes naturally. I have something in mind for you there," Marion says, "I think you will enjoy it. So that the other Directors can evaluate your performance with this task, I will be recording what occurs on skype and it will be transmitted onto that large screen on the wall."

One of Olivia's servants brings out a red long coat for Jillian which Jillian puts on.

When they are in the backseat of Olivia's car, Marion says to Jillian, "What is it that you fantasise about when you masturbate?"

"I don't know," says Jillian shyly.

"Yes you do," says Marion.

"Well maybe I like to imagine I am in a room naked and it turns out it is an art gallery exhibit and each visitor to the exhibit is invited to kiss me on part of my body and a succession of strangers kiss me on different parts of the body," Jillian says.

"Would you like to make that fantasy, a reality?" Marion says.

"Well it depends on what you have in mind," Jillian says.

"I quite often go to this place called the *Lookout*," Marion says, "It is kind of a well-known 'make out' place for the well-heeled who want to make love *en plein air*."

Jillian watches the pine forest from the window of Olivia's car.

There is a white full moon shining down on blue mountains. The road seems deserted until they turn off at a narrow road through the forest which winds around to a lookout where there are about seven cars parked with their windows fogged up.

Olivia's chauffeur parks the car next to a white Mercedes Benz SUV where an older man is seated kissing a woman and has his hand on her thigh. Jillian thinks that the woman looks familiar like someone she may have seen at Harrison Savings and Loan.

Marion turns to Jillian and says, "Jillian, could you please go to the car next door and tap on the window and ask if you can join them. If they accept you must insist on two things – firstly that the younger woman must be brought to orgasm first and secondly that the man must then accept being spanked on his bare buttocks by you and his girlfriend, each of you taking turns to slap each cheek."

Jillian has an incredulous look on her face and then shakes her head.

"If you fail to complete this task, then I will make a note of it for your file as unsatisfactory performance on a key performance indictor," Marion says.

Jillian smiles at Marion's comment, shakes her head and leaves the car, her bottom swaying under the red coat as she approaches the Mercedes.

Jillian leans forward and taps on the foggy window of the Mercedes.

Louis stops kissing his new girlfriend, Sarah and looks up and is surprised to see Olivia's beautiful young secretary, Jillian peering into the car, her breasts almost spilling out of her red coat. Louis cannot resist glancing at Jillian's cleavage. Louis winds down the window.

"Yes?" Louis says.

"Oh...sorry to interrupt," Jillian says hesitantly.

"Yes?" Louis says again.

"It was just..."

"I'm listening," Louis says.

"I wanted to ask if I could join you both?" Jillian says he face turning bright red.

Louis looks around and notices Olivia's car.

"Is Olivia in there?" Louis asks.

"No, no," Jillian says.

"Did Olivia ask you to come here?" Louis asks suspiciously.

"Why do you ask?"

"Well, I know you are Olivia's secretary. I remember you. I also know that is Olivia's car over there," Louis says.

"She's not there. You can look if you want to," Jillian says.

"To tell you the truth. I don't care if she is," Louis says with a grin, "What is it that you want to join?"

"Ah…I want to join you and your friend here," Jillian says.

"Why?" Louis asks.

"Why not?" Jillian answers truthfully.

Louis looks at Jillian searching her eyes for the truth. She knows that this is some game that Olivia is playing and that this beautiful young woman is just another pawn on the chessboard. *Hell, she is beautiful, though.* Louis looks over to Sarah who smiles a *yes.*

"I will let you join us on one condition," Louis says.

"And what is that?" Jillian asks.

"You will keep smiling that beautiful smile of yours," Louis says.

"I also have a request but I will tell you later," Jillian says.

"Anything for such a beautiful young secretary," Louis says.

"Come inside," Louis says and Jillian enters the back seat of the SUV.

"My name is Sarah," says Louis's girlfriend shaking Jillian's hand.

"Jillian," says Jillian.

"I'm not sure if you remember me. I'm Louis," Louis shakes Jillian's hand and she remembers seeing Louis in company photographs at Harrison Savings and Loan as a former director and still a major shareholder. Also she saw him leave Olivia's office before the shareholder meeting.

"Jillian, do you like to experiment?" Sarah asks.

"I… don't know," Jillian replies.

"What do you like?" Sarah smiles.

"Something different," Jillian answers.

"And why is that?" Louis asks.

"I want to experience more," Jillian answers.

"At my age, I just wanted to experience pleasure," Louis says, "If it feels good, do it. How's that for a philosophy of life?"

"Sounds good to me," Jillian says.

"Champagne?" Louis asks.

"Why not?" Jillian answers as Louis pours champagne into a champagne flute for Jillian and then one for Sarah.

"Did you come up here alone?" Louis asks.

"Another woman, Marion is here with me," Jillian answers.

"Well tell her to come over here and join us," Louis says.

Jillian leaves the car and taps on the window of Olivia's car.

"Marion?" Jillian says.

"How is it going?" Marion asks.

"They want you to join us," Jillian says.

"Well...OK," Marion says getting out of the car.

Marion introduces herself to Louis and Sarah and sits with Jillian in the back seat of the SUV.

"Champagne?" Louis asks.

"Is it French?" Marion queries.

"Of course, I would not buy anything but," Louis says with a laugh.

"Well I would be delighted Louis to accept a glass of your champagne," Marion says laughing.

"This is what I have in mind," Louis says, "Jillian will be my agent and do what I say when she is making love to you. Sarah will be Marion's agent and Marion will do what Sarah says while making love."

"Jillian, have you asked this man with very good taste in champagne about your request?" Marion asks.

"Well, we... ah... Louis here has agreed that I may make one request of him. I will let him know later," Jillian says.

Louis turns on the music in his car. It is a slow rumba. He kisses Sarah and runs his hand up along her leg, pushing the end of her dress higher and stroking her thigh with gentle strokes, seemingly oblivious to the two women in the backseat of the SUV.

"Jillian, as my first move I would like you to kiss Marion along the neck and then kiss her earlobes," Louis says, turning around to see how well Jillian performs her task.

"Well chosen," says Sarah.

Jillian leans in towards Marion and plants a soft kiss on Marion's neck. Marion smells of rose petals and her skin is smooth and soft. As Jillian kisses her, Marion closes her eyes in pleasure but does not say a word.

"If we are going to take it in turns, then why not make this a little more interesting," says Sarah.

"I'm listening," says Louis.

"Why don't we have a little bet together. If Marion brings Jillian here to orgasm first then you will be my slave for the weekend and if Jillian brings Marion to orgasm first then I will be your slave for the weekend. How does that sound?" Sarah says.

"Well, I would be quite happy for either of those eventualities so let us proceed. Your move?" says Louis.

"Marion, remove Jillian's top and bra and you do the same and then I would like you to rub your nipples together until I say stop," Sarah says.

Marion is pleased with the request and is already feeling turned on. She unbuttons her white blouse and then unhooks and removes her bra. Her breasts are full with long nipples that tilt upwards.

Marion then removes Jillian's shirt and bra. Marion then commences rubbing her nipples against Jillian's nipples until the nipples are erect.

"OK, now stop," Sarah says.

"Jillian I would like you to very slowly lick Marion's breasts from the base to the top and suck upon the nipples," Louis says.

Jillian follows Sarah's instruction, licking one breast and then the other follow with slow, deliberate strokes of her tongue. Marion's nipples reach even further skywards, a slow ache of pleasure building inside her.

"Touché, Louis," Sarah says, "Marion, please suck each of Jillian's fingers until each finger is wet."

Marion holds Jillian's slender arm up and kisses along the arm then starts to suck upon each of Jillian's fingers, moving her mouth up and down along the fingers, slowly while looking into Jillian's eyes.

"Jillian, please remove Marion's panties and slide two fingers into her vagina," Louis says.

Marion sits up slightly as Jillian reaches up under Marion's dress to remove her white lacy panties. Jillian then taps each of Marion's legs to prompt her to spread them wider.

Jillian's then edges two fingers into Marion's vagina. Marion is clearly already highly aroused. She closes her eyes and thrusts her pelvis in time with the movement of Jillian's fingers, Marion's breath becoming shallow and quick.

"I think we have a winner – me!" Louis says as Marion pants while coming hard.

"I have something very special in mind for you when we get home," says Louis.

"I can't wait," says Sarah.

"Excuse me," Jillian says, "I have a request for you as well."

"Well I think that is fair enough," Louis says, "What is it?"

"First, you need to get naked," Jillian says.

"This sounds promising," says Louis.

Louis removes his clothes. Louis is surprisingly fit looking for his age, the result of having spent many hours in his home gym.

"Now what? You let me ravish you?" Louis says with a smirk.

"Perhaps," says Jillian, "But first we must leave the car."

After all four get out of the SUV, Jillian says "Now please lean over the bonnet of the car."

Louis touches the cold metal of the car while Jillian whispers into Sarah's ear.

Sarah raises her hand in the air and swings it down upon Louis's right buttock leaving a red hand print surrounded by very white skin.

"Ouch. What was that for?" Louis asks.

Jillian then raises her hand up and smacks the other cheek so that there are now matching hand prints on each cheek.

"Should we take a photo?" laughs Sarah.

"I don't know. It's not something I could put on the mantelpiece," laughs Jillian.

"Hey, a man has feelings, you know," Louis says not really enjoying being the butt of the joke.

CHAPTER 11. THE TEMP

Jillian and Marion walk hand in hand from Olivia's car up the driveway of Olivia's mansion. They kiss each other goodnight and go to their rooms.

In the morning, Jillian finds an envelope with her name on it next to the bed with breakfast on a silver tray, three beautifully constructed *Le Chocolat* chocolates and a long stemmed red rose.

The note inside the envelope reads:

Dear Secretary,

You have completed each task required of you with aplomb so far.

Now for a real challenge. You are to be a temporary secretary at my office and must seduce all three of the management team and bring me an item of their underwear as proof.

A folio with their photographs and personal information is waiting for you in the car. To assist you in this task I have placed an outfit for you in the wardrobe. Good luck. Olivia's chauffeur will be waiting for you in her car.

Annika

Sun shines through the bathroom window as Jillian showers. She directs the warm spray of water from the showerhead between her legs while caressing her breasts with her free hand, thinking of her past adventures and the prospect of further adventures to come.

The outfit in the wardrobe consisted of a sheer black top, a white mid length skirt decorated with a pattern of red roses, a red coat, white stockings, lacy white panties, no bra and white high heeled shoes.

Jillian looks at her breasts in the mirror. They are full and shapely against the sheer black material. Jillian's lips are full and red and her eyes are dark and dramatic. Jillian imagines herself as a Bond girl given a secret mission.

The chauffeur nods to her and opens the car door for her. Next to her seat is a folio of information on each of the three members of Annika's management team at Union Energy.

The first photograph in the file is a large profile shot of a handsome middle-aged man named Stuart Patterson. His biography is rather mundane – divorced with three children who he sees on weekends. He enjoys playing golf, likes eating pizza and listening to commercial radio.

The next photograph is a thin woman with a birdlike face and wispy hair. The biography says her name is Roseanne Dean. She is single, a workaholic, and vegan.

The last photograph is a young man with curly black hair and thick black glasses. Jillian studies the photograph and thinks that a new haircut and some better frames would make him quite handsome. The biography says his name is Saul Dennison and he is a whiz kid in mathematics but has difficulty relating to people.

When Jillian arrives at the skyscraper where Union Energy is based she follows the instructions in the folder and goes to the fourteenth floor and asks for Ms. Dean at reception.

Roseanne Dean warmly shakes Jillian's hand and introduces her around the office and shows her the workstation that Jillian is to work from. Jillian is to provide secretarial support for Roseanne, Saul, and Stuart.

Saul is very shy when he meets Jillian and smiles briefly before looking down and disappearing into his office.

Stuart, on the other hand, is like the archetypal office *wolf* when he meets Jillian and shamelessly flirts with her, talking with Jillian for such a long period of time that Roseanne sees the need to interrupt them and show Jillian the staffroom.

Jillian thinks that it will be easy to seduce Stuart but exceptionally difficult to seduce Saul. Jillian thinks that Roseanne is too nice to seduce just for the sake of the silly games of the Emporia Club. Still a KPI is a KPI and Jillian does not want to disappoint Olivia.

At lunch, Jillian sits at a table by herself in the staffroom.

"Mind if I join you?" says Stuart with a rakish smile. Stuart has already deposited himself next to Jillian before she has a chance to speak.

Jillian giggles with Stuart's banter. The other staff cast disapproving glances towards them but they are completely oblivious to them.

Saul sits in a corner by himself facing a wall. Roseanne is at the gym.

Stuart jokes that Roseanne spends every lunchtime at the gym but after so many hours of exercise, has not managed to build a single muscle.

Stuart is so amazed at the reaction he is getting from Jillian with her eyelashes batting and her playing with her hair. Jillian is incredibly erotically appealing for him. Stuart whispers into Jillian's ear, "You are incredibly sexy Jillian. I have a luxury executive bathroom to myself. Would you like to see it?"

"Sure," Jillian says.

"I can sit on my thrown and see all of Manhattan," he jokes, "I would love to show it to you. Not me sitting on my throne but the view from the bathroom."

Jillian can't help but laugh at Stuart. He is so "on fire" for her and cute despite his weathered face and thinning hair.

"Well, I would love to see it," Jillian whispers back.

"Come on then," Stuart says

The bathroom really is impressive, thinks Jillian.

"This is really just to encourage us to stay in the office around the clock," Stuart says, " There's a television with cable, a toilet with gold accessories, marble tiling, a shower, fresh towels every day."

Jillian looks down at the other buildings and the ground is a beehive of interconnecting streets, yellow taxis, and people.

"It is quite hot in here with the sun coming down," Jillian says.

"Ah... yes," says Stuart. He has a look on his face like a man who is dying of thirst and has just seen an oasis.

Jillian's breasts curve deliciously upwards against the black sheer material of her top.

Stuart tries not to look at them while talking to Jillian but cannot resist glancing back towards her breasts.

As they talk Jillian steps closer to Stuart, looking deep into his eyes. Jillian appears to Stuart to be a beautiful angel, almost too perfect, like a vision from a dream. Her attraction is so wonderfully unexpected for Stuart.

Jillian kisses Stuart softly on the lips while looking into his eyes. Her fragrance is sandalwood, rose, and musk. She slides her hands up behind Stuart's back drawing him close to her so that he feels the warmth of her breasts pressed against his chest.

Jillian unbuttons Stuart's shirt and runs her hands over his chest while still kissing him. Her fingers encircle his nipples and she feels his erection pressing against his trousers.

Jillian strokes the erection over the trousers, then unzips the trousers and pulls Stuart's penis out and smiles at Stuart.

"Stroke it for me Stuart," Jillian whispers in his ear.

Stuart has never had this request before but starts to pull on his penis while shyly looking at Jillian and her beautiful breasts.

"Smack your butt," Jillian requests and Stuart lifts his hand and smacks it hard down upon his bottom and laughs.

"Well done," Jillian says with a half-smile playing upon her lips. *So this is how it feels to be in the driving seat.*

"Can you make it harder for me?" Jillian purrs.

Stuart more fervently strokes himself, his trousers bunched up above his shiny black business shoes.

"OK now sit on that chair over there," Jillian commands.

Stuart waddles over to the chair and sits down, his penis standing to attention like a souvenir Eiffel tower upon his lap.

"Put this on and don't make me wait," Jillian throws Stuart a condom from her handbag. He quickly unwraps it and places it over his erection.

Jillian quickly dispenses with her panties and pulls her dress up around her waist then swings one leg over Stuart and lowers herself down upon Stuart's tower. Jillian slides effortlessly up and down upon him while kissing his mouth and along his neck, still stroking his chest. It does not take long for Stuart to start groaning and bucking like a wild bull as he climaxes.

When he is spent, he partially comes to his senses. Stuart says, "I'm sorry Jillian. I don't know what came over me. You're just so damn gorgeous."

"That's OK, cowboy. I enjoyed it too," Jillian says, "There is one thing that you could do that would please me, though."

"Yes, anything," says Stuart.

"I would like to keep your underpants as a souvenir of today," Jillian says.

"That is a very unusual request. But of course, you can keep them," Stuart says. Stuart strips and removes his boxers and hands them to Jillian who folds them and puts them into her bag.

They shower together in the executive bathroom. Stuart's hands are all over Jillian's shapely body. Her mouth is warm and inviting and Stuart has a second erection, even harder and more intense than before.

"Well, hello," says Jillian, "Down boy."

Stuart kneels upon the shower floor and buries his face between Jillian's legs.

After the shower Jillian kisses Stuart on the cheek and strokes his face before she returns to her workstation.

CHAPTER 12. ROSEANNE À LA CARTE

Jillian determines that her next target for seduction is Roseanne, the pristine vegan. Jillian talks with Roseanne at every opportunity she gets – in the office kitchen, in the toilets and then invites her out for coffee in the café on the ground floor of the building.

"I'm new to this part of the city. Is there a good gym you know of around here?" Jillian says to Roseanne before taking a sip from her soy latte.

"Why yes there is – the one I go to," says Roseanne, "Would you like to come with me as a guest?"

"That would be fantastic," says Jillian.

"I'm going to go today after work," says Roseanne.

"Well, that would be great," Jillian says.

"OK, I'll come get you at 5pm," says Roseanne.

"Great. See you then," Jillian says with a smile.

Roseanne smiles back.

The gym is an all women gym decorated like a trendy nightclub with subdued lighting and a semi industrial design. The receptionist is bright and friendly and offers Roseanne and Jillian fresh wheat grass shots.

Roseanne has a very thin physique and works out with incredible intensity like she is training for a marathon or some other major feat of endurance.

Jillian does not even try and keep up with Roseanne in the spin class, on the treadmill or in the weights room. Just watching Roseanne makes her feel exhausted.

After the workout, Jillian and Roseanne have a drink then go to the change rooms.

Jillian peels off her skin tight yoga pants and small top in front of Roseanne and notices her glance in her direction before Jillian disappears into a shower cubicle.

"You are incredibly fit," Jillian says over the stall.

"You are very toned," Roseanne says back, "Do you work out often?"

"As much as I can," Jillian says.

"Are you hungry?" Roseanne asks.

"Famished," says Jillian.

"Do you care to join me for dinner? There's a fantastic sushi bar next door. They seat people in traditional Japanese style on the floor between these dividers. The food there is amazing," Roseanne says.

"I can't wait," Jillian says.

Jillian finds that the food really is amazing. The restaurant is so quiet that Jillian finds it hard to believe other people are eating around her. Their seats in the restaurant are surrounded by screens containing brush calligraphy from Japan.

Jillian fumbles with using her chopsticks.

"Let me help," Roseanne says holding Jillian's hand and showing her how to manipulate the chopsticks.

Jillian smiles and plants a quick kiss upon Roseanne's cheek.

"Woah...what are you doing?" Roseanne says.

"I just felt like it," Jillian says.

"Well, sorry. I don't go in for that type of thing," Roseanne says her cheeks blushing.

"What kind of thing?" Jillian asks playfully.

"*That* kind of thing," Roseanne responds.

"I think you just need to relax a little," Jillian says stroking Roseanne's cheek.

"You are a very pretty woman and you should be enjoying life a little," Jillian says.

"I do enjoy my life – thanks very much," Roseanne says.

"Well there's nothing wrong with sharing that enjoyment with someone else," Jillian says.

"Well I've never been kissed by a woman before," Roseanne says.

"Roseanne, I'm so sorry to hear that," Jillian says, "You're such an attractive woman. I have to say, I'm surprised."

"Well, thank you. You are very attractive as well but I'm straight," Roseanne says.

"Can I ask you something personal?" Jillian asks.

"You already know more about me than most people," Roseanne replies.

"Do you masturbate?" Jillian whispers.

"That is very personal. But, no - I don't," Roseanne says.

"You've never even tried?" Jillian says.

"No, never," Roseanne replies shyly, "I never felt the urge."

"Do you mind if I try something?" Jillian asks.

"What?"

"Just be patient with me. I need to check something," Jillian says as she brushes her knuckles along Roseanne's upper thigh causing Roseanne to flinch.

"I don't think this is a good idea," Roseanne says.

"Just be patient," Jillian says.

Jillian then lightly uses her fingertips to make small circles on Roseanne's leg then strokes Roseanne's cheek and Jillian then kisses Roseanne lightly on the lips.

Jillian looks into Roseanne's eyes which have a mild look of panic and confusion.

Jillian kisses Roseanne along her neck and then pulls Roseanne's blouse up from her skirt and touches the smooth, soft skin under the blouse very gently.

Roseanne closes her eyes.

Jillian unhooks Roseanne's bra and pulls it forward. Roseanne's breasts are like two firm apples with delicate pink areola.

In the background, two men can be heard talking in Japanese. Roseanne freezes for a moment then relaxes again as Jillian lightly caresses Roseanne's stomach and breasts, before removing her own blouse and bra and rubbing her nipples against Roseanne's nipples.

Jillian then reaches down between Roseanne's legs and with two fingers starts to rub in small circles around Roseanne's inner thighs, slowly reducing the circles until her fingers gently caress Roseanne's clitoris over her panties.

Roseanne's eyes remain closed, lost in the moment. She can feel herself starting to become aroused.

"Take off your panties and spread your legs," Jillian whispers into Roseanne's ear.

Roseanne follows this request, exposing herself to Jillian completely.

Jillian leans down and kisses in a circle around Roseanne's stomach before moving further down, licking in a long lick between Roseanne's legs then teasing and stimulating Roseanne's clitoris with her tongue while trying to make as little sound as possible.

Roseanne is so aroused that Jillian easily slides one then two then three fingers into Roseanne's vagina while still sucking and licking her clit.

Jillian uses her free hand to stimulate one of Roseanne's nipples after the other.

Roseanne's vagina then starts to contract around Jillian's fingers and she rocks her pelvic into Jillian's hand, trying to make as little noise as she can while orgasming in one intense wave of pleasure after another.

"Thank you, Jillian. That was amazing," Roseanne says breathlessly.

"Can I suggest you get a vibrator," Jillian says, "Once you learn what turns yourself on then you'll know how other people can turn you on."

"I'll do that," says Roseanne.

"Do you mind if I keep your panties as a souvenir?" Jillian asks.

"That's weird but I don't see why not," Roseanne says handing over her panties and for the rest of the day she enjoys the feeling of the freedom of not wearing panties and the sweet memory of her orgasm with the strange but beautiful secretary.

•

CHAPTER 13. EYE TO EYE

Jillian knows that Saul will be the most difficult person to seduce. He is difficult to talk to, let alone to get alone.

Nobody in the office knew much about Saul other than he is brilliant and reclusive. He works late. Jillian theorizes this is because he wants to leave after the rest of the office has left so he does not have to talk to people.

Jillian makes a point of staying back late, typing the annual report for the company as the office slowly clears of other people.

"Hello Saul," Jillian says as Saul emerges from his office.

"Hello... err, sorry I've forgotten your name. What is it again?"

Jillian is tempted to make a name up but then says "Jillian or Jill."

"Oh yes, Jill as in Jack and Jill, the nursery rhyme," Saul says looking embarrassed, hating himself for being so awkward around people, and around women, in particular.

"That's right. My proper name is Jillian but I let people I like call me Jill."

"My Dad wanted to call me Mars before I was born but luckily my Mum talked him out of it. He loved astronomy you see," Saul says.

Saul looks like he is about to make a B line for the exit when Jillian says, "What's your job here, Saul?"

"I deal with all the finances and also provide strategic advice to Annika, the CEO," Saul says, maintaining eye contact for a brief moment before looking off into the distance of the flickering office lights in buildings outside the window.

"Are you any good with computers?" Jillian says batting her long eyelashes.

"Well yes. My parents thought I might be addicted to them at one stage," Saul says with a smile, "What is the problem?"

"Oh, it's just that I'm trying to copy and paste some tables from the excel spreadsheets to the annual report and I keep losing all the formatting," Jillian says.

"I can help you with that," Saul says happily, coming over and looking at Jillian's screen.

"Is it OK if I drive?" Saul asks and Jillian smiles and gets out of her seat.

While Saul taps away on the keyboard, Jillian stands behind him and quietly removes all her clothes except her stockings, suspenders, and high black heels.

"You are amazingly good at this," Jillian says softly, before leaning over Saul so that her long hair falls upon him and kisses him on the forehead.

Saul's eyes look like they are going to burst from his head when he sees Jillian's beautiful naked form.

Jillian does not give him a chance to say anything but keeps kissing his mouth like she is an erotic vampire about to devour him.

Jillian leans over and unzips Saul's trousers and reaches in, pulling Saul's penis out and wrapping her hand around it, twisting around it and pulling it. Saul gets such a shock that he drops the computer mouse onto the floor.

Jillian then walks in front of him and bends forward at the waist to pick up the mouse. Jillian's perfect bottom is positioned right in front of Saul's face. Jillian grabs the mouse and runs it between her legs back and forth and then hands it to Saul who seems to have lost the power of speech.

Jillian then sits on her desk and opens her legs in front of Saul.

"Lick me," Jillian says.

Jillian feels one tentative kiss on her labia, followed by a tentative lick, then a long lick right between her legs then another one in quick succession.

Jillian thinks either he has done this before or he is a natural. She pushes against each lick that Saul does and he grabs Jillian's buttocks like he is holding a watermelon and sucking the sweet juice from it.

Saul then reaches his hands up and caresses and holds Jillian's breasts, encircling Jillian's nipples with his fingers.

Saul then takes out his throbbing manhood. Jillian passes him a condom from her handbag which he quickly puts on. Saul enters her, pushing deeply into her while Jillian uses one hand to stroke her clit.

Jillian's buttocks bounce against Saul with each thrust.

Jillian then wraps her legs around Saul's waist as he thrusts into her.

Jillian licks Saul's nipples in turn while he thrusts into her. The sensation sends Saul into overdrive until they are both a heaving mess.

Jillian looks at the computer screen and sees a long line of x's in the annual report where her bottom had been bumping against the keyboard.

"I like your style, Saul," Jillian says while kissing his cheek.

"Do you mind if I have your underwear as a souvenir?" Jillian says.

Saul just looks at Jillian with a smile. *Eye contact at last*, thinks Jillian.

CHAPTER 14. MIRANDA'S CHALLENGE

While in the back of Olivia's limousine Jillian thinks back over her sexual adventures. Jillian considers her options – does she "call time" on the Emporia Club's games or does she continue onwards.

These games have been intriguing, she thinks. They have allowed her to develop. To both surrender and control. To peel back the layers of conditioning to discover something honest, something utterly erotic, something animalistic, an urgent raw sexuality. She wonders - *where does this journey end?*

When Jillian arrives at Olivia's country mansion she goes straight with her trophies to the meeting room. The inner circle of the Emporia Club have congregated there in anticipation of her arrival. Jillian walks up to Annika and hands her a box containing the underwear of the three executives she has seduced.

Annika pulls each pair of underwear out and holds them out achieving a titter of laughter from the other women around the table.

"You have done very well, secretary," Annika says, "I am most pleased that you were able to achieve your KPI with those three."

"Your penultimate work task this week will be given to you by Miranda," Olivia says nodding her head to an African American woman in her thirties in expensive designer clothing.

Miranda stands up, walks over to Jillian and wordlessly hands her another envelope. Jillian quickly opens it and starts to read:

Dear secretary,

My challenge for you is to be my personal pet for one night - my cat.

Annika and Marion will prepare you for me.

Please return to your room and await their arrival.

Miranda

Jillian is not what is meant by "preparation" but assumes it will be something kinky.

Jillian turns and walks out the door to her room. She shuts the door behind her and sits on her bed.

Within five minutes there is a tap on the door. She opens it to see Annika and Marion. They both carry a bag.

"This is going to be amazing - très fantastique," says Marion.

"First, go have a shower. We will meet you in the bathroom after that," says Annika, patting Jillian on the bottom.

Annika and Marion stand watching Jillian as she undresses and takes a shower.

After Jillian steps out of the shower, she dries herself and sits down on a chair in the bathroom.

"Remove your towel for a moment," Annika says.

Jillian pulls away her towel and Annika and Marion inspect her.

"Your pubic hair is growing back, mon chéri," Marion says.

"Here is some shaving cream. Miranda likes her pets to be totally pubic hair free," Annika says.

Marion produces a shaver and proceeds to shave Jillian's pubic hair. She then applies a warm towel to the area to remove the shaving cream.

"OK, spread your legs to let me check," Marion says, tapping Jillian's leg.

Jillian opens her legs and Marion runs a finger over Jillian's labia and gently probes between the folds.

"Not bad work if I say so myself," Marion says.

"Miranda likes bright red lipstick. Could you put this on please," says Annika, handing Jillian a tube of lipstick.

Jillian applies the lipstick in the mirror then puts on her false eyelashes and does her eye makeup.

Annika runs her hands gently over Jillian's breasts then grabs hold of a nipple with each hand and gently pulls them until they are hard and erect.

"Make yourself wet for us," says Marion.

Jillian starts to stroke herself between her legs while Annika continues to play with Jillian's breasts.

When Marion sees Jillian's fingers start to moisten she says, "Put this in you," and hands Jillian a small silver egg shaped object.

"What is it?" Jillian asks.

"It's a vibrator - a remote control one," says Marion.

Jillian inserts the vibrator deep into her vagina while the two other women watch with interest.

Annika switches the vibrator on with the remote control.

"How does it feel?" asks Marion.

"Tingly," Jillian says.

"Now put these on and put this in behind," says Annika, handing Jillian black panties with a cutaway section at the back and a plug with a long black cat's tail.

Jillian pulls on the panties.

"Let me help," Annika says and squeezes some lubricant onto her hand and rubs it through the cutaway section of the panties.

"Try it now," says Annika.

Jillian eases the plug in behind.

"Now put this on," says Marion, handing Jillian a cat mask which covers the top half of her face. The mask has black pointed ears, a cat's nose with whiskers.

"And these, please," says Annika, handing Jillian four costume cat's paws, one for each hand and foot.

"Now, secretary, we would like you to walk on all fours. Miranda likes it that way," says Marion.

Jillian does not say anything but just nods.

"OK well get down on all fours," says Annika.

Jillian gets down onto the floor, her transformation complete.

"Follow Annika," says Marion.

Annika opens the door and walks down the corridor.

Jillian pads along on all fours, her bottom high in the air with the cat's tail moving as she crawls along, the vibrator buzzing in her vagina. The members of the Emporia Club stand and watch the strange sight of Jillian crawling along.

Annika turns the vibration level up to maximum with the remote control, causing Jillian to go weak at the knees.

Annika opens the door to Miranda's room. Jillian follows Annika in. Miranda is seated in a large leather lounge chair facing Jillian.

"What a beautiful pussy," says Miranda and the two other women leave the room after Annika hands Miranda the remote control.

Miranda walks around Jillian, inspecting her from every angle.

"You are a superb pussy," Miranda says, stroking Jillian's back like she is stroking the fur of a cat, "And your fur is so soft and silky. I have left out a plate of milk for you."

Jillian notices for the first time a saucer of milk next to Miranda's chair.

"Would you like a drink?" Miranda asks.

Jillian nods her head and then bends down to drink, her tongue lapping up the milk, with her pert bottom, high up in the air.

Marion runs her hands over Jillian's bottom, giving her buttocks a playful pinch.

"Look what I have for you. A bell!" says Miranda putting a collar with a bell on it around Jillian's neck. The collar has the name "Mittens" on it.

"I also have another present for you Mittens. A toy mouse!" says Miranda.

Jillian does her best to look pleased. Miranda throws the toy mouse to one corner of the room and Jillian crawls over to it on all fours and picks it up with her mouth and brings it back to Miranda who again stokes Jillian's back.

"Why thank you Mittens. You are a most well-behaved cat," Miranda says. "Now how do cats show their appreciation to their owners, Mittens?"

Jillian takes the hint and starts to rub her side against Miranda's legs.

"Now let's play with your pet mouse," Miranda says.

Jillian nods.

Miranda picks up the mouse and tosses it to the other side of her room.

Jillian crawls over, her tail swaying from side to side and picks the toy mouse up with her teeth. Miranda tosses the mouse again and they continue playing this game.

While Jillian crawls Miranda picks up the remote and experiments with different levels of vibration, slowly decreasing and then increasing the intensity of the vibrations to the maximum level until she can hear the vibrator buzzing away inside Jillian, who closes her eyes and makes a slight purr.

CHAPTER 15. ALL IN THE GAME

The inner circle all applaud as Jillian enters the meeting room.

Jillian has achieved all of the challenges set for her so far and has one final challenge to achieve.

Jillian does a slight bow and walks to the vacant chair around the table where there is an envelope marked 'Secretary'. Jillian opens the envelope and finds the following note:

Dear Secretary,

For your final challenge, you have a very difficult task. You are to seduce Antoinette Ward, your new boss and record it for me with your telephone. There is a file on Ms. Ward in my car for you to read on the way back to New York.

Good luck,

O.

This task makes Jillian pause for a moment as she weighs the risks involved in pursuing the final challenge.

Jillian then nods and leaves the meeting room at Olivia's mansion. All of the inner circle watch the big screen as Jillian enters Olivia's car and sits in the backseat and the driver takes Jillian back to New York.

"You are playing with fire, Olivia," Annika says.

As indicated, Jillian finds a file on the seat next to her in Olivia's limousine. There are a large number of news clippings about Antoinette and her interests, her history and her dalliances. Jillian reads that Olivia's current partner is Tina Scott.

There is also a credit card in Jillian's name with a post it note attached on which Olivia has written 'for expenses'.

"Take me to Bloomingdales," Jillian says to the driver.

In the expensive shopping centre, Jillian selects clothing from designers that Antoinette admires and then Jillian goes to the hairdresser and has her hair dyed red because it is noted in the file that Antoinette likes redheads.

The last purchase is two tickets to Don Giovanni at the Metropolitan Opera Centre, known to be Antoinette's favourite opera.

The following day, Jillian sits at the desk outside Antoinette's office.

"Good morning Ms. Ward," Jillian says as Antoinette walks to her office.

"Good morning Jillian. You look different," Antoinette says.

"You can call me Jill if you like. I'm trying out a new colour with my hair," Jillian says.

"I like it," Antoinette says before going into her office.

Later in the morning, Jillian answers the telephone,

"Welcome to Harrison. How may I help you?"

"Tina Scott here. Is Antoinette Ward there at the moment?"

"I'll just see," Jillian says then strums her hand on the desk for a few seconds and then returns to the call.

"No, I'm afraid she's not available at the moment. Can I take a message?" Jillian says.

"Oh, just let her know that Tina called. I'll be on my mobile," Tina says.

"Will do. Have a nice day," Jillian says.

Jillian lays the opera tickets out on her desk next to her handbag.

The next time Antoinette passes Jillian's desk she notices the tickets.

"Don Giovanni, a fantastic opera. Nice tickets as well I see. Celebrating something special?" Antoinette asks.

"Well I was going with a friend but she has bailed on me," Jillian says.

"That's a shame. Hey, I'll buy the ticket off you if you like. That opera is one of my favourites," Antoinette says.

"No I couldn't sell it to you but I would be more than pleased if you would be my guest," Jillian says sweetly.

"Well, I would be honoured. That's so kind of you. It's a date," Antoinette says.

Later in the day Tina calls back and says, "Hello, it's Tina Scott here again. Is Antoinette in now?"

"Oh sorry, Ms. Ward is out at present," Jillian says, "Would you like to leave a message?"

"Just tell Antoinette I called again. Thank you," Tina says, sounding quite frustrated, before hanging up the telephone.

"I will," Jillian says sweetly into the dial tone.

•

Thanks for reading! Please add a short review where you purchased this book and let us know what you thought!
Minuet Publishing[1]

[2]

---

1. http://minuetpublishing.wix.com/books

2. http://minuetpublishing.wix.com/books

Don't miss out!

Visit the website below and you can sign up to receive emails whenever Nicolas Blanc publishes a new book. There's no charge and no obligation.

https://books2read.com/r/B-A-IHVC-KDVK

BOOKS2READ

Connecting independent readers to independent writers.